D0764815

All as
Bright

All Is Bright

A COLLECTION OF TRUE CHRISTMAS STORIES

Anita STANSFIELD

Annette LYON

Gregg LUKE

H.B. MOORE

Julie WRIGHT

Kristen McKENDRY

Lynn C. JAYNES

Matthew BUCKLEY

Covenant Communications, Inc.

Cover image *Retro Christmas Banner* © Aleksandar Velasevic, 2009. Courtesy of iStock.
Cover design by Jessica A. Warner, copyrighted 2009 by Covenant Communications, Inc.

Published by Covenant Communications, Inc.
American Fork, Utah

Copyright © 2009 by Anita Stansfield, Annette Lyon, Gregg Luke, H.B. Moore, Julie Wright, Kristen McKendry, Lynn C. Jaynes, and Matthew Buckley

All rights reserved. No part of this book may be reproduced in any format or in any medium without the written permission of the publisher, Covenant Communications, Inc., P.O. Box 416, American Fork, UT 84003. This work is not an official publication of The Church of Jesus Christ of Latter-day Saints. The views expressed within this work are the sole responsibility of the author and do not necessarily reflect the position of The Church of Jesus Christ of Latter-day Saints, Covenant Communications, Inc., or any other entity.

Printed in The United States
First Printing: October 2009

16 15 14 13 12 11 10 09   10 9 8 7 6 5 4 3 2 1

ISBN-13 978-1-59811-906-0
ISBN-10 1-59811-906-0

Remembered at Christmas

KRISTEN McKENDRY

It was December in Canada—a wet, wind-whipped month that piled snow in sculpted drifts and encased tree branches in ice. I stood at the window, feeling like a hermit marooned in a cave—then again, with the way I was feeling, a padded cell might be a better metaphor. It had been a frazzling day. My three-year-old was irritable because we couldn't go to the park, and my eighteen-month-old was fractious with a fever. I was waiting anxiously for my husband to come home from work, worried about the long drive he had to make on treacherous highways to reach us.

It was three days before Christmas—another source of stress. My husband and I had been living in Canada for three years, but I still felt a keen homesickness for my family back in Utah, especially with the holidays approaching. Though I enjoyed our new home and didn't regret the move, there were times when the loneliness hit me particularly hard. I pictured my mother's hot chocolate, my family gathered around the piano to sing carols, and the beautiful crocheted ornaments on Mom's tree. I felt very isolated and left out. I knew almost no one in Canada. At times I felt I'd wandered so far away from home that even God had lost track of me.

It had been a difficult month leading up to the holidays. Since we had only one car and my husband had to take it to work, Christmas shopping wasn't much fun. I had to haul both children with me on the bus if I wanted to go anywhere on a weekday. And with my youngest, Ryan, feeling ill and the Canadian weather being, well, Canadian, I hadn't been able to get out of the house as much as I'd wanted.

I had had a particular present in mind for Ryan—one of those push toys that pops little balls around in a plastic bubble like popcorn as you push it. Ryan was an energetic, exuberant little boy, and I thought the cheerful popping noise and dancing balls would be great fun for him. I remembered having a toy like it when I was small. But I'd scoured every store I could think of and had had no luck locating one. There were lots of flashy, noisy toys—most requiring batteries or electricity—but no old-fashioned push toys. With Christmas looming near, I'd given up and come home with another present for him, but I was still disappointed. Really, it was a small thing, I felt myself grumbling, but couldn't even a *small* thing go smoothly in my life? Did everything always have to be such a struggle?

By the time my husband came home that afternoon, Ryan's condition had worsened. His fever would not come down. He had a history of having seizures when his fever spiked too fast, and I was anxious that it might happen again. We decided to go to the emergency department at the hospital as a precaution. Usually, whenever I rushed the kids to the doctor for some reason, it would turn out I had panicked for nothing; the kids were fine. So I was alarmed when the physician told us we'd been wise to bring him in and that he wanted to admit Ryan.

I hadn't expected this. I thought he'd just write a prescription and send us home. A hospital admission wasn't in my plans. I worked evenings at home as a phone operator for a pizza company, a job I hadn't had for long, so I quickly called my supervisor to let him know I wouldn't be able to work that evening. Thankfully, he was understanding, so my husband and I settled in to spend the evening with Ryan, getting him situated in his room in the pediatrics unit and trying to keep him and his brother entertained. Finally, I took my older son home and my husband stayed the night with Ryan.

The next day Ryan was diagnosed with a general staph infection, potentially serious but treatable. My husband and I spelled each other off throughout the day. That night I took the hospital shift, spending an uncomfortable night in a chair by Ryan's railed bed.

Hospital rooms are foreign and unfriendly places, despite the caring treatment of nurses with teddy bears on their scrubs. The smells, sounds, and hard surfaces all convey discomfort and illness, the sense that things are not right. My son was too unwell to really care where he was and too young to grasp what was happening. But I had an adult's knowledge of potential problems and a vivid imagination, and my anxiety and feelings of isolation only grew during those dark hours.

The next day Ryan began to respond to the antibiotics and started feeling well enough to become bored with lying in bed. I spent the day devising desperate little entertainments with plastic-cup pyramids and Kleenex puppets until I started to wonder if there was a bed available for me in the psychiatric unit, should I need it by the end of the day.

Christmas Eve came, and even though Ryan had improved somewhat, I was disappointed to learn that the doctor wanted to keep him at the hospital longer. We would not be home for Christmas. Once again I cancelled my shift, worried my boss would think I was making up excuses to get out of working on the one night no one wanted to work.

On what was supposed to be the most joyous of all nights, I was feeling sorry for myself. I couldn't help it. I was far from home, far from family, worried for my son, and wanted my mother so badly. And now we couldn't even have a proper Christmas dinner. All my plans were out the window. My husband and I sat in the hospital room, eating Kentucky Fried Chicken with the boys and trying to make the best of it.

Ryan was the only child left in the unit over Christmas. All the other kids were sent home. The halls were empty. The staff was cut to the bare minimum. Ryan seemed content and in good hands, and my husband and I were exhausted, so we decided we would both go home for the night, celebrate Christmas with our three-year-old, and return to the hospital in the morning.

Christmas Day, the Shriners, a charitable organization, sent a volunteer dressed as Santa Claus to the hospital to deliver presents to the children. But of course, Ryan was the only one there. I was surprised Santa had even bothered to stop by. The bright-costumed gentleman scared Ryan a little, so he didn't linger, but he gave a present to Ryan before he left—a push toy that popped little balls in a plastic bubble as you pushed it.

I couldn't believe it. I had searched everywhere for just that toy, and here it was, delivered by "Santa" himself. As I watched my son toddle happily up and down the hospital halls with his noisy popper, I felt my weariness and sadness fade away, and I was filled with a strong sense of comfort. I knew God's hand was in my life. I might be far from home and in a worrisome situation, but I wasn't alone or overlooked after all. I hadn't been forgotten. I knew my wishes for a push toy to give to Ryan were not particularly important, especially in comparison to my wishes for his recovery. But Heavenly Father knew the secret and silly desires of my heart. What was important to me was important to Him. And He cared enough to acknowledge those desires of my heart with that simple gift.

With tears in my eyes, I turned to my husband, but my heart was too full to express what I was feeling. I could only manage, "See? Someone knows we're here."

My husband just smiled and replied, "Yes. But is it God or the Shriners?"

Being Santa

JULIE WRIGHT

She crept up behind me and asked me a question that halted me mid-pan-scrub.

I am a terrible liar. I get all flustery and red when I try to fib. And I am not the Grinch. My heart is not two sizes too small. And my shoes fit just fine. I'd always loved Christmas—Santa Claus; packages; warm, comforting smells from the kitchen—I loved it. All of it. And then I had *her*.

The lines between right and wrong and of good parenting seemed blurry with a child of my own, especially at Christmastime. Did I buy into the lie of a guy in fancy red pajamas breaking into houses to deliver presents? Or did I teach her the Christmas story of a stable, shepherds, and a baby?

Could I do both—cross my fingers behind my back and not count the little tale of the guy in red as a fib? I had avoided the issue by simply not stating one way or the other when it came to the reality of the fat guy in a red suit. I figured when the kids were old enough to ask outright, I'd fess up to the truth. Until then, I'd just avoid it all. *Avoidance* was a vital part of my parenting toolbox. It had served me well until that day of dishes and the question.

"Is Santa Claus real?"

Oy. I pulled my hands from the sink and methodically wiped them on a dish towel, my mind spinning for a good answer to that particular question—one that didn't implicate me as the bad guy.

I bent down and stared at my four-year-old, her big hazel eyes wide with suspicion and accusation. "What do you think?" Hedging questions by placing them on the other party usually worked when it came to topic avoidance.

She wasn't having any of that, though. Her wide eyes narrowed, and her little hands went to her hips. It bothered me that she looked a lot like me when she did that. "I asked *you*."

I couldn't lie. But I couldn't tell the truth either. In a moment of decision, I removed one of her hands from her hips so I could hold it and walked her to the coat rack, pulling both her jacket and mine off the hooks.

"Well? Is he real?"

"Let's go for a walk." I opened the front door to the cold, gray-drenched landscape outside and led her across the street to the hair salon.

As we pushed the door open and stamped the snow from our shoes, she said, "Mo-om!" in that plaintive voice that meant she was tired of being put off.

"Just give me a minute." I scanned over the snowflakes taped to the window. Genders, ages, and wishes were found on each white piece of paper.

I told her what the snowflakes said and asked her which one she wanted to pick. Puzzled and still looking suspicious, she pointed to one. We pulled it free from the window and headed to the store.

"Mo-om! I asked a question!"

"Yes, you did. Just give me a minute." Stalling was another important part of my parenting toolbox, kept in the same general area as avoidance and hedging. The ability to explain complicated situations has always evaded me. It isn't that I don't know the answers, but it's hard for me to explain that knowledge to other people. And that's why I found myself wandering the store in search of the doll requested on the paper snowflake. I couldn't explain Santa Claus. I had to show her.

She picked out the doll and the wrapping she wanted to use, and we went home to wrap the gift. "Is he real, Mom?"

"Be a good girl and hand me the tape pieces. I'll answer your question in a minute."

She did as instructed, babbling about how the little girl who got this doll would love it because it came with hair jewels that could be used in real hair too. She placed a small finger on the ribbon while I tied the bow. "Are you not telling me because you don't know? 'Cause I can go ask Dad." I'd have been offended by such a statement if it weren't for the fact that her dad really did know a lot about everything. We went back out to the hair salon to drop off the present.

Once we were back out in the cold and walking home I asked, "Do you know what you just did?"

"I gave a present."

"Yes. You gave a present. You were Santa Claus for someone."

She stopped in the middle of the road. "What?"

I tugged at her hand. Stalling wasn't such a good tool when your child stood in the middle of the road. "You were Santa Claus. Santa Claus isn't any one person. He isn't a guy with a beard who slides down chimneys. Lots of people get to play Santa Claus for Christmas. Your dad and I get to be Santa for you and your brothers. And sometimes, when there are people who are having hard times, other people get to be Santa for them, like you were just now for a little girl you don't know and might not ever meet."

"Has someone ever been Santa for you?"

I thought back to several years earlier, when things had been hard and finances tight. We'd found a basket on our porch filled with things we needed, and even a few things we just wanted. "Yes. Someone has been Santa for me."

"I like being Santa." She pulled harder on my hand and started to run. "Let's get the boys so they can be Santa too!" I had to stop her and tell her we had to wait until the boys actually *asked* about Santa before we could tell them.

I felt pretty good about the whole situation and patted myself on the back. Self-congratulation doesn't get out of the parenting toolbox very often, so I like to soak in it when the opportunity arises.

It was three or four days later when my daughter came back with a statement rather than a question. I was doing laundry this time. "Heavenly Father is Santa Claus."

"What?" I mentally slapped my forehead. She still didn't get it. I thought I'd done a good job explaining the Santa situation, but it seemed I'd ended up confusing her even more. I should have told the truth, let her feel betrayed and have a good cry, and be done with the whole business.

"Heavenly Father gave us Jesus. That's a really good present. He's a better Santa Claus than even me." She skipped off, leaving me standing stunned with a pair of mismatched socks in my hands.

With eyes stinging from tears, I glanced at the Nativity scene on top of the bookshelf. I dropped the socks back to the pile and wandered over to pick up the little carved manger with a baby in it.

> For unto us a child is born, unto us a son is given: and the government shall be upon his shoulder: and his name shall be called Wonderful, Counsellor, The mighty God, The everlasting Father, The Prince of Peace. (Isaiah 9:6)

Every moment of my life requires that gift given on the first Christmas. A baby in a manger who grew to be exactly what every person in the world needed. Yes, Heavenly Father is a better Santa Claus than even me. Often when things are hard, that gift Heavenly Father gave has wrapped around me and whispered, "Peace unto you . . . Merry Christmas."

Goodwill Toward One

ANNETTE LYON

I'd known Susan* only a few weeks when I walked into a rehearsal that June afternoon for the community youth play she was directing. We rehearsed at a local library, usually with the cast on the blue multileveled carpeting of the multipurpose room and Susan sitting on a table in front. This afternoon, however, things were obviously different. She still sat on the table, but even I could tell from her puffy eyes and the hair sticking up in twenty directions—hair she'd been pulling chunks of as she paced the room during practice—that something was wrong. Plus, the typical wide smile and sparkle in her eyes were gone.

When the cast filtered out the door at the end of rehearsal, Steve and Michael, twins, who—like me—were about to embark on their senior year of high school, rushed to her side and asked what was wrong. I stayed back a bit, hovering, not wanting to pry. The boys had known Susan from a play the previous summer and considered her a close friend. At seventeen and a half, I was the oldest cast member, and aside from the musical director, Susan was the only adult present.

With a twin on either side of her, Susan burst into tears. Both hands pulled at her short hair again, and this time black rivulets of mascara traced down her cheeks. "My husband left us," she croaked out. "I don't know what we're going to do." My stomach dropped to my toes. How could a father of five children just leave? I was amazed that Susan had held it together as well as she had during rehearsal.

"He won't pay the mortgage, so we'll have to find a place to live. I don't have any money, and until the divorce is final, he won't give me a dime."

As teenagers, we didn't know the first thing to say to comfort Susan, but we hugged her close—and I think we drove her and her kids, who were also in the play, home, because she'd been running low on gas and had gotten a ride to the library to save what pennies she still had. When we arrived, she and her kids got out of the car with sad little waves. Instead of our usual teenage banter and silliness, we drove home in somber silence.

As the summer wore on, we watched Susan and her children struggle and become increasingly desperate for money. We could see the physical and emotional strain on their faces as her soon-to-be ex-husband withheld money for even the basics of life. Susan shared few details, but it didn't take many clues to figure out that her finances bordered on terrifying. Several people suggested she quit the play and let someone else direct it. She refused, saying that the play was the one thing keeping her sane in the turmoil.

And I think it did—she brought joy to the young cast, the sparkle in her eyes gradually returning as the play progressed and the actors and dancers learned their parts. Every time someone nailed a solo, or a dance number went just right, she'd pull chunks of hair—only in joy—and hop off the table, crying, "Yes!" Her joy rubbed off on us, and ours rubbed back off on her. It was a reciprocal way of surviving the summer for her.

When the play ended in the fall, several of the older cast members and I kept in touch with Susan and followed what happened to her young family. Her oldest daughter, Tammy, was so angry that she refused to even speak to her dad. As expected, Susan and the kids had to move out of their home when the mortgage wasn't paid. She found an old, run-down building to live in. It looked like a house from the outside, but at some point—likely decades ago—the inside had been remodeled into a business office. Her stake president was the landlord and let her have the place for a low rent.

So Susan moved her kids into a place with peeling paint, a kitchen that consisted of nothing but shelves and a sink, and a drinking fountain in the hall. It even had separate men's and women's bathrooms. The only real plus was that her two sons enjoyed having a urinal.

Months passed, and Susan's situation grew worse. She and her stake president/landlord exchanged negative words. He placed some blame for the separation on Susan. She expressed anger and hatred toward her ex-husband. Somehow in the middle of the tragedy, he took away her temple recommend. Susan was devastated. The one place she could go to feel of God's love for her, to find peace and answers, was taken away from her. Her anger and hatred toward her stake president built to a crescendo.

As a result, Susan resented her landlord—and stake president—more each day. She despised sleeping in his "house" and living on his charity but had nowhere else to go. She could hardly feed her children. She was looking for work, but aside from directing community theater periodically, she'd been a stay-at-home mom for nearly twenty years. She couldn't find solid work that could provide for a family of six, and she had to beg her ex to provide anything. I suspect that by this point the court had ordered at least some child support, but he was still holding out.

Worse, Christmas was coming. At this rate, they wouldn't even have a tree. I was approaching my eighteenth birthday and felt entirely helpless. I might technically have been an adult in a few days, but what could a high school senior do? I felt terrible about the situation, but about all I could realistically do was say a periodic prayer for Susan.

At this time, Steve, Michael, and I were participating in our high school choir. During the month of December, we held a benefit concert to raise money and canned goods for the local Sub for Santa program. As we sorted through the donations and goods at the end of the benefit, we were amazed to find that the donations from the concert exceeded the needs of the families our school had been selected to help.

Left over were five stockings, a big box of canned goods, and a couple hundred dollars. Steve, Michael, and I knew exactly what to do with the extra. We felt the surplus had been provided by someone above—we even had the right number of stockings. Our choir teacher gave us the money and the cardboard box of canned goods for Susan's family.

About half a dozen of us from the old cast sat down and wrote a list of Susan's children's names and ages, along with what we knew about them. One daughter would love some earrings. The two boys adored bowling but hadn't had a chance to play since the divorce because they couldn't afford it. We knew the oldest daughter wanted some new clothes. And so on. Then we went shopping, scouring the mall sales racks and doing all we could to stretch those dollars as far as they could go. We got several gifts for each child, including a gift certificate to the local bowling alley.

Now the trick was figuring out how to get all the gifts and the box of food into the house without the family knowing.

We enlisted the help of a dear friend of Susan's. He agreed to take Susan and the children out one evening to see the Christmas lights on Temple Square, and while they were gone, we'd be elves and sneak into their home to deliver the gifts. Steve had visited Susan earlier that day and had secretly unlocked a window so we could get in.

That night, as a carload of teenagers, we giggled excitedly as we drove up to the aging building where Susan lived. The windows were dark; no one was home. Steve killed the engine, got out of the car, and jogged to the unlocked window. He shoved. It wouldn't budge. He shoved harder with his shoulder. Nothing. The window was so old it was stuck shut. Several others in the group tried to force it open, but to no avail.

Now what?

"Wait!" Michael said. "Tammy couldn't go with them tonight because she had to work."

"So?" I asked. What did that have to do with getting into the house?

"So, what if we go to the restaurant where she works, get her keys out of her purse, and use them to open the door?"

It sounded like a long shot, but it was our only hope. We couldn't very well leave all the gifts on the front steps for anyone to take.

We piled back into the car and drove to the restaurant. Steve sneaked inside and found the manager, hoping Tammy wouldn't see him. Amazingly, the manager not only believed his story but got Tammy's keys from her purse and handed them over.

Steve emerged from the restaurant triumphant with Tammy's key chain held aloft. We whooped and hollered—then remembered to quiet down—and zipped back to the house. We'd lost a good half hour and didn't know how soon Susan would return. We went into a flurry of elving. The box of food—covered with holiday paper—went by the front door. Gifts were arranged on the couch. The stockings were lined along the closed piano lid.

As a final touch, we lit a pot of potpourri on the piano then crammed ourselves back into the car, wishing we could see the family's reactions when they saw what we had done. Steve sneaked back into the restaurant, returned Tammy's keys to the manager with a big thanks, and swore her to secrecy. We drove home feeling lighter than air.

A day or two later, we delivered a Christmas tree to Susan that one of the cast members' parents had bought for her. We helped her set up the tree in the makeshift living room. As we stood back and admired it, Susan became teary-eyed.

"You guys will never believe what happened," she told us.

This was our moment of truth—could we maintain poker faces? It turned out that as our theater director, Susan had taught us how to act well—no one batted an eye or threw a knowing glance at anyone else.

"Oh, really?" we asked. "What?"

Her kids were bouncing around, trying to show off their gifts. We noted a familiar sweater and a pair of earrings. The boys were waving a piece of paper like a flag in the air.

Watching them, Susan covered her mouth, trying to hold back emotion, and sat on the couch. She gathered us around her and described what had happened after she and the children had come home from seeing the lights—the sight of the gifts and food and stockings nearly bowling them over. The kids had opened the gifts even though it wasn't Christmas yet.

"Whoever did this knew our family. They knew the kids' ages and sizes, their interests—they even knew that the boys love to bowl. Who in the *world* could have known that?"

She never suspected us; we were a bunch of broke teenagers; of course we couldn't have bought all this stuff. We expressed wonder and amazement—and somehow kept the truth from showing on our faces.

"The door was locked when we left—I know it was," Susan said with a shake of her head. "*How* did they get in?"

We were supposed *to get in through a window,* I thought wryly.

"The only person outside our family with a key is my stake president." Her face crumpled, and another tear rolled down her cheek, taking mascara with it. "I can't see how it could have been anyone else. If he did this for us, then I've misjudged him. I need to be kinder from now on. He's not perfect, but then, neither am I." She tapped her chest. "I need to find a way to forgive him. I still think he was wrong to take away my recommend, but he's human. We all make mistakes. And he was doing the best he could. I shouldn't harbor such anger against him. He's . . . he's a good man."

A reverent silence fell over the room, and no one wanted to break it by speaking. Susan's heart had been softened.

I blinked back tears, knowing that the secret of Susan's miracle needed to be preserved, that there was a reason our choir had just enough stockings left over, just one more case of food, and just enough money to buy presents for her family. Susan's Father in Heaven knew she needed this moment to soften her heart and allow peace and forgiveness inside.

Giving her stake president and landlord the credit for the miracle wasn't the point—forgiveness and peace was. Our little theater group was simply fortunate enough to be in the right place at the right time to be instruments in the Lord's hands in making it happen. For the first time in months, Susan was able to feel forgiveness and peace instead of anger and resentment.

I didn't see as much of Susan over the next year, but I know that a good deal of healing went on. She got back on her feet financially and was able to find a better place to live with her children. She gradually healed from the wounds her ex-husband had caused. She eventually remarried. To my knowledge, she never again said a negative word about her stake president.

The gift Susan received that year wasn't just cans of green beans, a sweater for her daughter, or a few games of bowling for her sons.

Forgiveness—that's what Susan got for Christmas.

For months, she'd lived in a dark, miserable place full of bitterness and despair. It was a situation not of her own making, thrust upon her by someone else's actions. But it had been eating her alive from the inside out. She was finally able to feel some peace with the thought that one person out there was better than she'd assumed, that the same someone cared about her, and that it was worth letting go of one piece of bitterness weighing down her spirit.

In the end, Susan received what the Christmas season is supposed to be about—peace on earth, goodwill toward men.

Or at least toward one man. And that was enough for one year.

Names have been changed.

A Christmas Story

H.B. MOORE

Any good Christmas story must have several ingredients—the story of the Savior's birth, a human heart changed, faith renewed, or faith restored—all intermixed to lift our spirits and teach us what the Lord desires us to know. My Christmas story is perhaps one that you might not expect, but it's one that forever changed who I am.

I have walked where the Savior walked. I have looked over the waters of the Sea of Galilee and watched the fishermen cast their nets. I have visited the Garden of Gethsemane and walked among the ancient olive trees. I have stood on the hill of Golgotha, the site of His crucifixion, overlooking the city of Jerusalem.

But more than this, I have learned that whether or not you or I have visited the physical places where the Savior lived, we must all come to understand who He is in our hearts.

Months after I proudly earned my driver's license in Utah, my family moved to Israel in August 1987. It was no surprise. In fact, the summer before when my father first learned of the opportunity to teach for a year at the BYU Center in Jerusalem, he asked us to fast and pray as a family. So we did, and we all felt "good" about the decision. But I soon discovered that making a decision at fifteen and living that decision at sixteen were two different things.

Entering my junior year of high school in a new school, I quickly drew attention. I was the "new girl," the American. The private Anglican school that I attended was in downtown Jerusalem, and my younger brother and sister and I took a bus from our apartment to the school each day. Passing through neighborhoods of Orthodox Jewish families, we swiftly learned that if we wanted to wear shorts to school, we had to change after we got off the bus. Modesty was taken to the next level in this country. The local Orthodox Jewish women covered from their ankles up to their wrists. My sister and I also soon discovered that unless we wanted to be sitting by a twenty-something-year-old Israeli soldier carrying a loaded AK-47, we had to sit together, which left my brother to share a seat with a soldier many times.

My high school class was small—only nineteen students were in my grade. It didn't take long for the questions to come once they found out that I was a Mormon. I wore a U2 T-shirt like any average American girl, and when my new friends noticed, they immediately wondered if I was "religious." Religious? I didn't understand. Did I go to church? Yes. I'd been a Mormon my whole life, lived in an average city in Utah, and hadn't really committed any wrongs besides fighting with my sister. Yet here in a foreign country, I was suddenly faced with questions on the status of my faith.

In time, the puzzle pieces came together. I learned that other Mormons who had gone to that school hadn't exactly lived the values that members of our faith claim to uphold. When my classmates had seen the rock-band insignia, they had equated a rock-band fan with someone who also enjoyed things that a rock star did—such as drinking alcohol. So my new friends wanted to know on which side of the fence I sat. They wanted to know if I was a faithful Mormon or if I had strayed from Mormon values.

It was one of the defining moments in my life when I realized that I needed to make a decision. Would I represent my faith and stand as a witness, or would I go along with the often inappropriate behavior of many other teenagers?

I thought back to when I'd received my patriarchal blessing just months before. I had fasted all night and day—until about the only thing I had energy to do was sleep. But I had made it to the home of the patriarch with my family. During the blessing, I distinctly remember wondering how the patriarch could know so much about me. But even more powerful was the presence of the Spirit and the emotions that flooded through me.

Remembering this experience brought back the same emotions and the same assurance that the Lord had testified to *me* of the truthfulness of His gospel. I couldn't deny it.

Coming from the average Utah neighborhood, I had yet to face real temptation. All of my friends were on the straight and narrow like I was. The boys I'd dated so far had been respectful. I had attended many youth firesides where the main topic seemed to be "peer pressure." It made me laugh sometimes because I was certainly independent. No one was going to tell me what to do or force me to do anything I didn't want to do.

But the questions suddenly pressed on me: What *did* I want? Who was I? And what choices did I need to make to get where I wanted to go? These were weighty questions for my sixteen-year-old mind, but as I was thrust into the spotlight at this new school, I couldn't hide behind my Mormon friends, or even my parents, any longer.

October came, and one of the lovely benefits of living in the midst of a Jewish community was that school was let out for two weeks to commemorate Sukkot—a Jewish holiday. My family and I traveled about the countryside, visiting the Sea of Galilee and Nazareth. One day we traveled to the Arab town of Bethlehem. The town was a bustling tourist spot, and we were bombarded by street sellers before entering the cool, dark Church of the Nativity, which was built over the "holy site" of Christ's birth.

Ducking to enter through the four-foot-high doorway, I was first struck by the gloomy lighting and then the smell of incense. Every section of the church was claimed by a different Christian religion—each with its own icons and collections of burning candles. We followed a group down the stairs until we reached a small room underground—a room that was believed to be the cave in which the animals had been kept. It was quite dank, but the atmosphere was quiet, reverent somehow.

The room narrowed into a small stone alcove where a silver star had been nailed to the marble floor. An iron rail separated the location of the star from the pressing onlookers. The star, placed by the Roman Catholic Church in 1717, marked the location where Christ's manger had supposedly stood. I looked around at the group of people and marveled how we could all come from different countries, hold different faiths, yet still be in the same room with the same thoughts.

I watched as others bowed before the grotto and kissed the ground. Some took pictures. Others seemed to be meditating. I stood there, waiting for an epiphany of sorts. *I'm here,* I thought. *This is where the Savior Himself was born, fulfilling thousands of years of prophecies.*

*Bringing to fulfillment the law of sacrifice. Redeeming all of mankind.
Now what?*

Still, I watched the others, more focused on their actions than the
shiny symbol of the past on the floor. The tourists continued milling
about, some leaving, more arriving. Words were whispered, but
mostly there was silence accompanied by the sound of quiet shuffling.

Soon, it was time to go. We ascended the stone steps that took us
to the altar of the church and then stepped back outside into the
glaring sunlight. Cars honked, tourists bustled, and children younger
than me held up souvenirs to sell. *How can this be one of the holiest
spots in the world?* I wondered as we skirted a group of police officers
who were blocking off a smoking car. Whether the smoke was caused
by a bomb or some stray tear gas, we didn't stay around long enough
to find out. Tourists started moving to their buses—Bethlehem was
closing for the day, and curfew was near.

As we drove back to Jerusalem along the windy, narrow road, I
thought about that silver star and the church that had been erected
above it. I wondered why I hadn't been bowled over by the Spirit. I
had expected an experience similar to the one I'd had when receiving
my patriarchal blessing. All at once, the answer seemed simple. The
truth of the gospel was not a place. It was a state of being.

My life in Jerusalem moved steadily forward, but this epiphany
remained in the back of my mind, giving me the foundation I needed
when faced with temptations. On the weekends, I'd meet my friends
"in town," where the bustle of nightlife attracted many groups of
teenagers. There were no age restrictions at the local clubs, and a
sixteen-year-old American girl could order alcohol as well as any
adult. It was quite amusing that my friends would say no for me.
Whenever a new person would join our table and offer to pay for a
round of drinks, one of my friends would pipe up and say, "Oh, she
doesn't drink. She's religious." I was overwhelmed by the respect my
friends had shown me and how peer pressure was turned on its ugly
head. I realized that the Lord had blessed me with new friends—
friends who were willing to stick up for *me*. Although they came from
various backgrounds, they accepted my differences.

December came—a time when religious pilgrims from all over the
world congregate at Jerusalem, and more specifically, Bethlehem.
Candlelight services are held all week long leading up to Christmas Day.

My family accompanied the BYU student group to a location just outside of Bethlehem to avoid the tourist menagerie. There are several hillsides that are termed affectionately "Shepherd's Hill," even if from year to year the actual location of the hill changes for different student groups.

Sitting on the hillside among the olive trees and listening to the bleating of the nearby flock of sheep, I felt as if time stood still. The sun set upon the cool evening as the BYU students stood one by one, testifying of the Savior. I listened with half an ear, the other part of me dwelling upon the city in the distance—Bethlehem. It wasn't hard to imagine what it might have been like on that night when the angel brought good news to the shepherds. At first, they were afraid. And until the angel told them to fear not, for the news he brought was "good tidings of great joy," the shepherds didn't know how to react (Luke 2:10).

What impressed me the most was that they overcame their fear and believed. Then they put their beliefs into action. They didn't doubt or question but hurried into Bethlehem to visit Mary, Joseph, and the newborn Child. And they didn't stop there. After they had seen the Savior, the shepherds "made known abroad the saying which was told them concerning this child" (Luke 2:17). They testified of Christ in only the way humble shepherds could: by sharing their personal witnesses. That was something I could do through my choices around my school friends. By what I said or how I acted, I would essentially be sharing my beliefs.

Night was drawing close, and I gazed across the landscape as the town of Bethlehem started to light up. At that very moment, I realized I *was* a witness too. An angel wasn't standing before me, but I was surrounded by those who were testifying of Christ, just as the angel had done two thousand years before.

Did I have to actually see an angel or the Christ child myself to be a witness? Just two years before, Elder Bruce R. McConkie had said something that has never left me: "I am one of his witnesses, and in a coming day I shall feel the nail marks in his hands and in his feet and shall wet his feet with my tears. But I shall not know any better then than I know now that he is God's Almighty Son, that he is our Savior and Redeemer, and that salvation comes in and through his atoning blood and in no other way" ("The Purifying Power of Gethsemane," *Ensign,* May 1985, 9).

Whether sitting on a hillside overlooking Bethlehem or trudging through the dusty back roads of Nazareth or gazing across the Sea of Galilee, I knew that my testimony of the Savior and the true meaning of Christmas didn't come from my surroundings but from within. Like Elder McConkie, I didn't need to see the Savior Himself to have faith in Him and act as a witness. It didn't matter whether I'd walked where Christ had walked or seen the place where He had been born, but it did matter *how* I lived. Although Christmas may only come once a year, the influence of the Savior affects me every day. I have come to understand that my choices do make a difference. My choices have become my witness to the world.

The Christmas We Lost Our Barn

**JOHN DAVIDSON'S TRUE STORY
AS TOLD BY GREGG LUKE**

I was only four years old at the time, but the memory of that cold December day in 1967 will stay with me forever. We had worked very hard that year building our herds, maintaining our ranch, and harvesting enough hay to see our livestock through another long Wyoming winter. We owned 640 acres about seven miles southwest of Lyman. We had our house, the huge old barn, a garage that was used as a tack and storage building, a machine shop, and several other outbuildings. I was the only boy and the youngest in a family of five children; still, I tried to pull my own weight as best I could. My father was a hardworking, generous man. As a former bishop of our ward and owner of the local grocery-mercantile store, he never ceased to help people, whether spiritually or materially. The whole family took turns helping out around the ranch as well as in the mercantile. We were never what you would call rich; everything we had was invested in the ranch and store. But because of Dad's selfless service, everyone in town and the surrounding area knew and respected the entire Davidson family. Despite not having much ourselves, during Christmastime it was not unusual for us to play Secret Santa, giving gifts to several needy families. Helping people in need always brought a warm feeling to my heart and taught me that the true spirit of Christmas is about giving.

Ranching our barren, unforgiving land was hard, never-ending work, but always very rewarding. That spring and summer had been better than most; we ended up with a good hay crop and several new calves, lambs, and foals. But winter seemed to come quicker than usual that year, entirely skipping fall. I remember the cold being particularly harsh. The wind never ceased from howling, and needle-sharp ice crystals pelted any exposed skin. The ground had frozen solid as granite. We kept our cattle, sheep, and horses near our barn to make it easier to feed them through the winter months and to guard them from predators and exposure to the bitter cold.

We had 250 head of cattle inside the barn, and we worked the calves in there too, dehorning, branding, and vaccinating them for the season. We also stacked much of our hay inside and around the barn—some 17,000 bales. The rest of the crop was nestled between the barn and the adjacent building.

On the morning of December 12th, my sisters Susan, Linda, and Sheri had gone to school, and my older sister Colleen had stopped by for a visit. She was married and was pregnant with her first child. Dad had taken a young bull over to a neighbor's ranch and had spent most of the morning there, helping with the neighbor's milk cows and other stock. He had said he was also going to stop by the lumberyard for some fencing materials. I was wandering about the house as usual, wishing my sisters would come home so we could play. It was too cold to do much outside, but I was very bored and restless and willing to do just about anything. I went to the back door to look outside, just in case the sun had broken through and warmed the yard a bit. At that moment, flickers of orange and yellow caught my eye. They came from the top of our big barn. The flickers were flames. Fire!

I ran to Mom, yelling that I had seen a fire in the old barn. At first she thought I was fooling, but the panic in my voice convinced her to look outside. She gasped and immediately called the fire department. She told Colleen to keep me inside as she ran out to see what she could save from the flames. The inside of the barn was an inferno. The animals were bellowing violently, driven mad by the fire. Many of the horses and calves were already dead. Mom ran to the adjacent building and was able to save a few saddles and other bits of tack, but she only made it in and out once before the fire had engulfed that building too. She came back into the house, shaken and drawn. Colleen and I watched the flames from our kitchen window as Mom paced about the house, letting out small gasps and bursts of tears.

Within minutes several big red fire trucks and farm pickups arrived. They sprayed some water on the blaze, but by then it was too late. All they could do was prevent the flames from reaching our house. Time seemed to drag on as we watched the hopeless battle.

Men and machines were moving everywhere, and steam and water covered the whole yard, but nothing was able to stop the relentless flames from attacking every building on our homestead. It was horrible. While the men worked outside, the women did their best to console my mom inside our house. Even though I thought the big fire trucks with their high-pressure hoses and loud, rumbling engines were pretty neat, I had trouble being excited about them. Mom was trembling and crying, and seeing her so sad caused tears to stream from my own eyes. Not only was this tragedy devastating to my family, but I somehow knew it would also ruin Christmas—now just a couple of weeks away.

Meanwhile, Mr. Anderson, a teacher at Susan's school, found Susan in the hallway and took her to the office. He told her something terrible had happened at home. Susan called home, and Mom told her about the fire and that her favorite horse had died in the flames. Susan was too shocked to say much more than okay and good-bye. She hung up, but Mom called back to make sure she was okay and explained in more detail what had happened. Susan decided to finish the day at school since no one was able to pick her up. She later said that riding home on the bus with my sister Linda seemed surreal—as if they were in a slow-motion dream. When they got home, the only structure still standing was the house. Every other building had burned to smoldering heaps of debris.

When Dad came home, he just wandered about the yard with his hands in his pockets. He said he had seen the smoke from the lumberyard and had commented to the lumberman that a person would have to be crazy to start such a big fire on such a windy day. A moment later, a friend had pulled up and told Dad that his place was on fire. Dad had driven home as fast as he could.

Seeing Dad in the yard, I ran out to see if I could help. As I approached him, I saw that his face was covered with tears, some frozen, some still trickling down his cheeks. Earlier that week, Dad had shared with me a portion of his patriarchal blessing that said as long as he obeyed the commandments and was faithful in his Church callings, his family would never want for anything. Just as I reached his side, he looked toward heaven and said, "Lord, I don't know how you're going to do it this time."

Dad had just purchased a new International Tractor. It too had been stored in the barn. The tractor was so new that Dad hadn't had the chance to get it insured and hadn't even made the first payment on it. It was totally destroyed. In sifting through the debris, Colleen found a Dutch oven in which Dad had kept a collection of silver dollars he'd acquired at the store. It was now a solid lump with random impressions of eagles, the word *Liberty,* and partial coin edges on its surface.

The rest of the day was a blur. People showed up with food items and such, but we were still in too much shock to do anything but stare and cry.

I don't remember Dad—or any member of my family—asking for help, but the very next day, trucks, tractors, and bulldozers showed up and began pushing the charred rubble into piles to be hauled away. The work was amazingly organized for such short notice. As soon as the ground was cleared, the men measured the land for a new barn. Because the ground had frozen solid again, they placed old tires where the barn posts would need to go and set them on fire. The tires burned all night and thawed the ground enough for the men to sink sticks of dynamite into the ground to blow through the frost line. Someone always seemed to be working on the barn, and every day someone would drop off several bales of hay to feed our remaining stock. During that time, the community rallied around us as never before. It was as if our world had completely fallen apart, and everyone else was working to put it back together again. One morning we found a Jersey milk cow tied outside our back door so we wouldn't have to buy milk. Other gifts of that sort showed up all winter long, including several tons of hay for our cattle. One kind, elderly man gave us a gentle old mare named Gypsy. She was a wonderful gift that kept our minds off the loss of our other horses.

The work crew finished the barn on Christmas Eve—just twelve days after the old one had burned to the ground. On Christmas morning there was a huge red ribbon tied around the barn and a big sign tacked to the large double doors that read MERRY CHRISTMAS!

It was overwhelming to see how the community had come forward to donate food, livestock, lumber, hay and feed, handfuls of money, and, of course, hours and hours of time. We were never able to calculate the total amount of money the labor and gifts equaled, but we knew it was a debt we could never repay. And the thing was, no one expected us to.

The Christmas our barn burned down will always stay rooted in my memory—not as a heartache or a tragedy, but as the perfect example of generosity, sacrifice, and love. It was the year my family got the chance to be on the receiving end of the true spirit of Christmas.

The Candy Bucket

MATTHEW BUCKLEY & ROBIN JENSEN

Author's Note: Matthew Buckley is my pen name. My real name is Marion Jensen, and I was named after my grandfather. He died before I was born, and I know him only through his journals and the stories told about him by my uncles and aunts. This is a true story of a Christmas shortly after my grandfather returned from World War II in 1945.

The children attached to the three noses on the windowpane could have sworn they smelled the wet snowfall outside. They had been watching the snow fall most of the afternoon, thinking about Christmas. Would Santa come? And if he did, what would he bring? In recent years, Dad had been away at war, and even though Santa had come, the gifts he'd brought had been more practical than fun. Their hopes this year—now that Dad was back *and* had a job—were greater than they had been in years.

From behind them came Dad's voice. "David, run out behind the house and bring in the old washtub. You know, the one with the hole in it."

Dad had returned home from the navy four months earlier and, because he had been in the South Pacific, was still tan and dark. His black hair, which had recently been cut short to meet naval regulations, was only now beginning to grow longer than the quarter inch he had worn it at then. In contrast to his hair and complexion, his eyes were an icy blue that seemed to twinkle when he was happy.

David, the oldest at eight, ran to obey his father. Dad rounded up Michael, who was four, and Cathy, who was five, and took them to the front room by the Christmas tree.

When David returned with the tub, Dad tousled his sandy hair and brought out one of Mom's old stockings and a pair of scissors from deep in his overalls pocket.

Whispering low, he said, "We're going to play a trick on old Santa Claus this year, kids. Do you want to help me?"

"How are you going to do that, Dad? Does Mom know about this?" asked Mike.

"Is it safe?" said Cathy.

David added, "You can't do that, Dad. You can't trick Santa. He knows everything."

"No, kids," said Dad. "Santa's getting old and probably hasn't had time to get his eyes checked this year. I bet he's half blind and won't be able to see what we're going to do."

"What are you going to do, Dad?" Mike asked.

"Well, I'll tell you what. I'm going to hang Mom's old nylon stocking here on the mantel. Underneath that I'm going to put the old washtub. Then I'm going to cut a hole in the toe of Mom's stocking and let it hang into the tub. When Santa starts to fill my stocking, he won't see the candy falling into the tub. He'll keep trying to fill my stocking until the tub is full."

Without waiting for the children to respond, Dad cut the hole, hung the stocking, and positioned the tub. When he was finished, Mike, who had been the quietest throughout the proceedings asked, "Dad, if your trick on Santa works, will you share your candy?"

Mike was surprised by Dad's reply. "Sure, I will. In fact, I'll get so much candy that you might as well not even hang your stockings. I'll get so much that if we split it four ways, we'll all get sick."

The silence that greeted this suggestion was long. Finally it was determined that the three children would still hang their own stockings—not to be greedy, but so that if Dad's idea worked, they would be able to give the candy in their stockings to Mom and still share with Dad. Dad agreed.

On Christmas Eve the family read the traditional scriptures and watched the lights on the tree. The children hoped that by some seasonal magic, Santa really had received their Christmas messages. Eventually, everyone was sent to bed.

It can't be said that David, Cathy, and Mike dreamed of sugarplums. The three of them had never seen one. But they certainly had visions of snow, trees, and gifts. And most assuredly they dreamed of a tub full of candy. Maybe even the whole corner of the room would be filled with more candy than they had ever seen. Dreams like these are enough to keep a child asleep for a long time. When the light of the morning came, however, two parents found themselves being watched by three sets of sleepless eyes.

As Mom opened her eyes, the children grew bolder and approached the bed.

"Do we have to eat first?" asked Cathy.

"I want to save room for my candy," said Mike.

"Can we just go in the other room and see?" asked David.

The rush of questions woke Dad, who said, "Come on, kids. Let's go see how much candy we tricked out of old Santa." They retreated to the dining room, and when the folding doors were opened, they were met with the sights and smells of Christmas.

All eyes turned to the mantel, searching for the mountain of candy in the tub. But rather than being filled to the brim with sweets and goodies, the tub was full of coal. There was a small bit of kindling and a note on top. The children looked at their stockings. Each one was full, bursting with nuts, candies, and fruit. All, that is, except Dad's nylon stocking. It was hanging there empty of any Christmas joy. Dad went over to the tub, picked up the note, and read it out loud.

> *Dear Mr. Jensen,*
> *What am I to do with you? Trying to play a trick on old Santa. What I have left you is what you deserve. Please try to be a better example to your children.*
> *Love, Santa.*

Dad wadded up the paper, threw it on the grate, took some kindling from his tub, and started the fire.

None of the children dared say anything. None of them reminded their father that they were going to give their stockings to Mom and share Dad's candy. And oh how they were relieved that they had left up their stockings. If Santa was going to do things that way, they were glad it had been done to their dad and not to them.

The fire began to warm the chilly air, and soon the happy sounds of Christmas filled the room.

It was good to have their father home this Christmas. The last two years without him had been quiet and lonely. To have joy and happiness and fun together, as well as treats, was all the Christmas season should be. And even though Dad's trick hadn't worked, it had been fun to dream about.

Through the rest of the day, when no one was looking, each of the children slipped Dad a little of their candy. And through the rest of the day, though no one was looking, Dad would smile and put piece after piece of coal on the fire.

The Ghost of Charles Dickens

ANITA STANSFIELD

Dickens is dead, to begin with. There can be absolutely no doubt about that. It's not that I personally have any evidence of his demise. I was not around to see the body or to attest to the fact that he had been physically alive and subsequently dead. However, I trust the historical accounts of many reliable individuals who have reported the details of the death of Charles Dickens, followed by his burial at Westminster Abbey. I can certainly make a logical assessment based on simple facts to assure myself that he is, indeed, dead. Dickens died in 1870, so it's not likely that he somehow faked his death as a joke and has been in hiding all these years. I must reasonably conclude, then, that Dickens is dead. And yet, the spirit of his work continues to delightfully haunt this world, especially at Christmastime.

A Christmas Carol, in one form or another, has been a part of my Christmas celebrations from my earliest memories. My father struggled with chronic depression, and there were times when it was very difficult to make him smile or to even see a hint of a pleasant expression. But I remember well how he enjoyed watching those old black-and-white versions of *A Christmas Carol* and how they would make him smile, sometimes chuckle. I had no comprehension at the time of how gifted Dickens was at delicately interlacing humor with pathos. He could tug your heartstrings, frighten you, and make you laugh, all in a matter of minutes. While I was well aware of the story and its popularity through my childhood, it wasn't until 1980 that *A Christmas Carol* touched my heart, jumping from its previously passive position to one of the most prominent aspects of celebrating the greatest event in history.

I had been married only a couple of months as we settled fully into the Christmas season. It was a year of many firsts. Among them was crossing a line that put me into a closer realm with my two older sisters, who had both been married for many years. The two of them lived close to each other and did many things together, and now that I'd left the single and dating category, we became more of a threesome. On a Saturday a couple of weeks before Christmas, my sisters invited me to attend a matinee of a film version of *A Christmas Carol* that they'd seen in the theater the year before. It was titled simply *Scrooge,* and it starred Albert Finney. When I heard it was a musical, I felt a little skeptical, but my sisters both gave rave reviews that encouraged me.

My new husband was working that day, and I went to one sister's home before the movie to make banana bread that I intended to give as Christmas gifts to friends. While my sister and I worked together in the kitchen, with some of our favorite Christmas music playing in the next room, we talked and laughed and shared memories of our childhood Christmases. We were looking forward to the traditional Christmas Day brunch at our parents' home, knowing that even though we were all adults, Santa would still be filling our stockings that hung on the fireplace in the living room where we had spent our childhood. By the time the banana bread came out of the oven, it was time to go.

One of the most distinct memories I have of that day was the fog. I'd spent my entire life in Utah Valley, and I'd never seen such fog. It had settled over the valley and remained there for weeks. It made driving difficult, especially after dark, and many people complained. But I liked it. I felt as if I'd been transported to London. I didn't make the connection at the time, but now I think it was somehow fitting that my memorable Dickens experience that day was surrounded by fog. Dickens wrote a great deal about fog, and he used it both to set the mood and to create metaphors. So, this day has maintained a kind of magical sense in my memory, enhanced by the fog that seemed to hold all of the present realities and concerns in life at a distance. I was content to just be surrounded by fog that seemed a tangible representation of the Christmas spirit in the air. Barely into adulthood, I hadn't spent any time pondering the desire to hold onto that magical feeling of Christmas that was such a big part of my childhood. But I remember feeling it that day.

As we settled into the theater with our popcorn and other treats, a musical overture began to play that went on for several minutes before the film actually began with the ringing of many bells. What followed had very little similarity to any film version of the classic tale that I had seen previously. It was full of vibrancy and celebration! The story that I had grown up with took on more depth and meaning in this unique presentation. While honoring Dickens's story very well, the music was clearly inspired and added a magic to the story that I'd never experienced before. I became utterly engrossed with characters I had believed I'd known well, but I was now seeing deeper into their experiences. There was something about this version that emotionally tugged my heart into the profound depth that I know Dickens intended but had often been skimmed over. I'd never before realized how truly poor Bob Cratchit and his family were or how deeply damaged Ebenezer Scrooge had been from his childhood. I'd never before noticed that it was a story that illustrated the stark comparison between wealth and poverty and the injustice that took place when those who had more than enough were unwilling to share with those who were suffering.

I learned through passing years, as my fascination with *A Christmas Carol* grew, that much of Dickens's own sufferings and struggles were laced into this story. He'd suffered many hardships in his childhood, and he'd known both abject poverty and wondrous wealth. But the poverty had forever scarred him. No matter how much money he made, he felt afraid of losing it and of forcing his family into the horrors of workhouses and debtor's prison that he'd endured as a child. I believe Dickens saw a little of himself in Scrooge and that Scrooge's change of heart expressed an ideal that Dickens himself would have liked to achieve. But whatever other messages may have been woven into the tapestry of this story, the blazing glory of it is clear and simple. The truest theme of *A Christmas Carol* is rooted in the most simple and basic Christian truths. Be kind to all people. Give of yourself. Share what you have to ease the suffering of others. And of course, remember that it's possible for men to change and to put their pain behind them. And yet these messages are so delicately intertwined that their presence is one of the elements that classifies this story as a masterpiece. The very fact that the story does not boldly declare Christianity and yet continually implies Christlike values allows people everywhere to comfortably receive the story's timeless and universal messages.

As a writer, I have pondered and analyzed this great work over and over, and the absolute inspired genius of it always leaves me in awe. But the real power behind the story is something that's difficult to analyze, and I first felt it that Saturday in 1980 as I sat there in the theater, utterly mesmerized and transported to another realm. I'll never forget the feelings that filled and surrounded me as the film ended: a stark contrast of disappointment that the movie was over, and a hovering residue of the Christmas spirit that connected the tender memories of my childhood to the hopes and dreams of a new life before me. It was dusk when we came out of the theater, and the fog had become heavier. But I loved the mystical sense it gave our surroundings, which helped me hold onto the magic I had felt.

After leaving the theater, we went to a local bed and breakfast that was a restored Victorian home. The establishment had started a tradition of having a Christmas open house. Together my sisters and I explored the beautiful mansion's exquisitely decorated rooms as if we were children. The Christmas decor added a magical appearance to the already-lovely Victorian furnishings and accents. I recall that the house smelled like Christmas, and it was easy for my imaginative brain to conjure up possibilities of what might have taken place inside these walls in decades past. Christmas music was being played on a beautiful grand piano in the parlor, and pleasant refreshments were served. While taking in the magic of *this* experience, the wonder of the movie we'd just seen remained with me, and yet I had no comprehension of how the impressions of that day would impact my life and my work. Nearly three decades later, I can look back and see how something both creative and spiritual was awakened in me that day. My fascination with Dickens and his works has blossomed recently, and I've found myself learning a great deal about life *and* writing by studying what is written by him and about him.

To my knowledge, *Scrooge* didn't play in the theater anymore after that year, and our desire to repeat the experience eluded us. However, over the years, watching the DVD has become an integral part of my family's Christmas celebrations. The tree, the scented candles, the Nativity, the carols, the family activities, the food, and *Scrooge*. I play it over and over. It accompanies me while I wrap gifts, decorate, and clean house. It's usually the first movie of the season that I watch and the last.

My adult life has been filled with many struggles and challenges as well as many joys. My husband and I share five children now who are moving into adulthood and starting their own families. But the first Christmas gift my married children received was a DVD copy of the musical *Scrooge*. And the kids all agree: Christmas just wouldn't be Christmas without the music, the humor, the tenderness, and the messages of this film filling the house. Of course, the true meaning of Christmas is the most prevalent aspect of our celebrations, just as living a Christ-centered life is something I try to focus on every day, and I strive to make teaching my children the lessons of life my highest priority. And that's just the point. The messages of *A Christmas Carol* echo my deepest beliefs, not just at Christmas, but always. Because I've come to know the story so well, there are lines of dialogue that often resonate in my mind or even pass through my lips at moments when they seem to be teaching me something related to whatever might be happening in my life. The most prominent of those has become a part of my daily life: "Mankind should be our business." These words help me keep perspective when there are so many different pressures tugging at me from all sides. The messages of the story remind me that being there for others in need should be my highest priority.

I look forward to meeting Charles Dickens someday, or maybe I already have. I like to imagine the possibility that we both belonged to some organization of writers before we were born to this earth life, that we encouraged each other in our creative endeavors. Either way, I know our inspiration comes from the same source, and I hope to one day have the privilege of personally thanking Him for the personal suffering He endured in order to create a story that would impact my world more than any other piece of fiction.

I realize that Charles Dickens is dead. There can be absolutely no doubt about that. But while his spirit lives on in another realm, his work endures as a testament of his deepest beliefs. And I gratefully add my own by echoing his words: "God bless us, every one."

Follow Your Star

LYNN C. JAYNES

"Yes, the larger Christmas story is clearly not over. It is not solely about some other time, some other place, and some other people. It is still unfolding, and we are in it!"

—NEAL A. MAXWELL, *THE CHRISTMAS SCENE,* © 1994 BOOKCRAFT, INC.

"You bought what?"

"I know it sounds silly, but it'll be a good thing. You wait and see." It was dark when we loaded the five-foot Barbie dollhouse into my husband's pickup. Was he was rolling his eyes? I was sure he was rolling his eyes. Not that I blamed him. It even sounded silly to me. What was a fifty-year-old woman doing buying a dollhouse? But it was all part of "following my Christmas star," I just knew it. Sort of. Maybe. But it's awkward explaining the intricacies of following a Christmas star to someone without sounding just a tad crazy. Let's back up a bit, though. We read this about the original star-followers:

> Now when Jesus was born in Bethlehem of Judaea
> in the days of Herod the king, behold, there came
> wise men from the east to Jerusalem, Saying, Where
> is he that is born King of the Jews? for we have seen
> his star in the east, and are come to worship him.
> (Matthew 2:1–2)

It seems a little odd to me that only the Wise Men saw the star. Or perhaps only the Wise Men followed the star. Then again, maybe only the Wise Men knew what the star signified.

> When Herod the king had heard these things, he
> was troubled, and all Jerusalem with him. (Matthew
> 2:3)

Ah-ha! So they did know what the star signified.

> And when he had gathered all the chief priests and
> scribes of the people together, he demanded of them
> where Christ should be born. And they said unto
> him, In Bethlehem of Judaea: for thus it is written
> by the prophet, And thou Bethlehem, in the land of
> Juda, art not the least among the princes of Juda: for
> out of thee shall come a Governor, that shall rule my
> people Israel. (Matthew 2:4–6)

At this point it would seem the Wise Men *told* Herod of the star
and brought others into the loop as well. But, as far as we know, the
Wise Men were the only ones who went looking for the Christ child.
Odd.

> Then Herod, when he had privily called the wise
> men, enquired of them diligently what time the star
> appeared. And he sent them to Bethlehem, and said,
> Go and search diligently for the young child; and
> when ye have found him, bring me word again, that
> I may come and worship him also. When they had
> heard the king, they departed; and, lo, the star,
> which they saw in the east, went before them, till it
> came and stood over where the young child was.
> When they saw the star, they rejoiced with exceeding
> great joy. And when they were come into the house,
> they saw the young child with Mary his mother, and
> fell down, and worshipped him: and when they had
> opened their treasures, they presented unto him
> gifts; gold, and frankincense, and myrrh. And being
> warned of God in a dream that they should not
> return to Herod, they departed into their own
> country another way. (Matthew 2:7–12)

I don't know why others didn't follow the star. I don't know what they saw or didn't see, what they knew or didn't know. All I know is that the Wise Men followed the star and that it ultimately brought them to Christ. One thing this story teaches is that the purest way to worship Christ is to identify and follow His star, which will lead us to Him. I've seen wise men and women on earth who have followed stars, but they didn't ride camels and didn't bear gifts of myrrh and probably couldn't even spell frankincense—certainly couldn't afford gold. Their names and gifts were not exotic but rather ordinary. I've learned a great deal from modern-day "wise men" who drew closer to Christ by finding and following their own Christmas stars.

I'll tell you about one of these wise men. One year at the beginning of the Christmas season, my friend Tracey told me about an e-mail that had circulated at her work, asking for volunteers to ring the bell for Salvation Army donations. She was surprised by the request, assuming that bell ringers were usually people somehow connected with the organization. She considered the request, but because she wasn't connected in any official way to the Salvation Army, she didn't respond to the e-mail. After all, her daughter had a birthday party on the same day. How could she do both? She didn't give it another thought.

As the appointed bell-ringing day drew closer, another e-mail was sent asking for a volunteer. Tracey mulled it over but, well, surely someone else would volunteer. Yet the thought nagged her until finally Tracey "saw the star" and recognized what it signified. The next morning she called the person who had sent the e-mail. Was he still looking for someone to help? He was. Tracey called her husband and gave him a choice—either ring the bell or supervise the birthday party. He chose the birthday party. At that point Tracey "followed her star" and rang the bell.

Tracey told me about her experience ringing the bell in the cold. She told of the things she learned and observed, of the people who greeted her, and of those who refused to make eye contact. With gracious tears she described the demeanor of those she had met and her own humbled attitudes and perceptions. In short, her star had brought her to Christlike service and to greater love and appreciation for her fellow man. Her star had brought her closer to Christ.

I want to be a wise woman, and I'm working on it. I looked in some of the usual places—picking up the shopping-list ornaments from trees in department stores, donating toys to charity bins, dropping a few coins into collection boxes, and joining organizations in providing canned goods to families in need. While all of these activities were good and brought a measure of satisfaction, it wasn't until I *really looked* in some not-so-obvious places that I found my star—a role that perhaps I alone could fill, that would bring me closer to Christ. Hence, I was now the owner of a five-foot-tall Barbie dollhouse.

The star appeared so early in the season that I almost didn't recognize it. It came in November. A coworker told me she had a dollhouse she wanted to sell. It was five feet tall, in great shape, and had all kinds of accessories—tables and chairs, a refrigerator that opened with food on the shelves, a baby's layette, pictures to hang on the walls, couches, beds, and all sorts of knickknacks. It was a very expensive set, and she was willing to let it go for a fraction of its original cost. As she described the dollhouse to me, I felt something. And I saw something—the star. So I told her I'd buy it.

On the drive home that night, I questioned my star sighting. I wondered if this was actually the star or not. Maybe I had misread the signs. What was I thinking? I had no idea what to do with this dollhouse. I knew no one who could use it. I tried to justify the purchase by convincing myself that simply buying it was enough—maybe the coworker just needed a little cash boost and this was the way to do it. But that didn't feel quite right.

The dollhouse was an even bigger dilemma to explain to my husband. After all, where would we put a five-foot dollhouse? Our only granddaughter was still in diapers two thousand miles away and was more interested in dogs, horses, and her bottle than dolls. We had three grandsons and were expecting a fourth in February, but grandsons do not play with Barbie dolls. I thought about repainting the house with green and brown camouflage colors and stocking it with a few G.I. Joe action figures. My backup plan was to haul the dollhouse to Deseret Industries before the bishops and Relief Society presidents went there to shop for Christmas gifts to give to families in need. But I hated to do that. It felt like a cop-out. It seemed like a Wise Man making his way to Jerusalem and then sending an emissary to bear his gift to Bethlehem. That wouldn't do. I wanted to come closer to Christ, not send someone else to do it for me. The more I thought about it, the more I knew that I had seen the star and that there must be some purpose for it, even if clouds were momentarily blocking its light. I wondered if this confusion was what the Wise Men might have felt when they showed up in Jerusalem and had to ask for directions. I needed directions.

I decided to call the Relief Society president in our ward and ask if she could help me out. When she told me she didn't know of anyone who needed a dollhouse in our ward, I almost gave up. Following this star was not easy. I began to feel a little silly; I had bought a ridiculously large dollhouse and hadn't the faintest clue what to do with it. I would just have to wait until the star shone a bit brighter.

I was still trying to figure things out a few days later when a woman who knew of my dilemma tapped me on the shoulder. Did I still have the dollhouse? Why, indeed I did. She knew of a family who could use it, and she arranged for the family to pick it up at my house. It was a family I hadn't seen in years, and I had lost track of the children and their genders and ages. We arranged a time for the parents to pick up the dollhouse. At the appointed time, the parents came and were very gracious and grateful. There, I told myself. The deed was done. I supposed I should have felt overjoyed that the dollhouse had found a home. I should have had warm fuzzy feelings. But I was mostly just happy that the burden had been lifted and that my conscience was lighter.

The next morning, my husband and I were out and about and happened to catch sight of the same family who picked up the dollhouse. The whole family. There was the mom, the dad, two boys, and—most remarkably—four little girls. All under the age of ten.

> And, lo, the star, which they saw in the east, went before them, till it came and stood over where the young child was. (Matthew 2:9)

Four little girls. I had no doubt the star had pointed the way to this sweet family that needed a five-foot-tall dollhouse. My gift had found its home. I sat in awe and wonderment, feeling a small portion of the warmth the Wise Men must have felt. I too had come closer to Christ by following the light of a star.

Every Christmas now, I look for the star. I'm anxious to see what adventure it will bring me this year.